The Movie Storybook

Adapted by Michael J Flexer

Pencils by Lawrence Hamashima

Paintings by Koelsch Studios

First published in Great Britain by HarperCollins Children's Books in 2008

HarperCollins Children's Books is an imprint of HarperCollins Publishers Ltd,

77-85 Fulham Palace Road, Hammersmith, London W6 8JB.

A CIP catalogue record for this title is available from the British Library. No part of this publication may be reproduced,

stored in a retrieval system or transmitted in any form or by any means, electronic, mechanical, photocopying, recording or otherwise,

without the prior permission of HarperCollins Publishers Ltd, 77-85 Fulham Palace Road, Hammersmith, W6 8JB.

The HarperCollins website address is: www.harpercollinschildrensbooks.co.uk

All rights reserved.

ISBN-13: 978-0-00-728436-8

Madagascar TM and © 2008 DreamWorks Animation L.L.C.

1 3 5 7 9 10 8 6 4 2

Printed and bound in Italy by Rotolito Lombarda S.p.A.

HarperCollins *Children's Books*

Alakay the lion cub was playing in Africa with his father - a powerful lion called Zuba.

But little Alakay wandered away from his father and into the clutches of two poachers. The poor cub was locked in a cage and thrown on to the back of a truck. Zuba gave chase to rescue Alakay but a shot from a poacher's rifle sent him collapsing to the ground. When the truck turned a sharp corner, the cage flew off and splashed into a surging river.

'Da da?' murmured baby Alex as he was carried away by the current and out across the sea to New York City and the New York City Zoo. But that was a long time ago...

Today, Alex was excited to be leaving Madagascar and heading back to Manhattan with Marty, Melman and Gloria.

The plan was to fly back in an old warplane repaired and piloted by the penguins. As the four pals climbed the steps to the plane waving goodbye to their lemur friends, King Julien burst out of a cake. 'Surprise freaks! You will be very glad to hear that I am coming with you,' he declared.

Finally, the rickety plane creaked along the runway. 'Sit back, relax and pray to your personal god that this hunk o' junk flies.' Skipper announced.

BON VOYAGE

It wasn't long before a little red light started blinking in the cockpit.

'Rico. Manual,' ordered Skipper.

Rico handed him the manual and Skipper smashed the light. 'Problem solved,' he announced as the plane ran out of fuel.

'Aaaahhhh!' screamed the New Yorkers as the plane plummeted downwards.

Then ... THUMP!! Suddenly, the plane smashed into some treetops, skidded off a cliff and crashed to the ground.

Alex, Marty, Melman and Gloria emerged from the plane and stared at a beautiful valley full of animals.

'Africa,' sighed Marty. 'Our ancestral crib.'

But the animals' reverie was broken by the appearance of a terrifying lion. It was the leader of the pride and he thought that Alex wanted to challenge him.

'No – no challenge,' Alex stuttered, waving his paw in what he hoped was a friendly fashion.

From behind the large lion stepped Florrie, a female lion. She couldn't take her eyes off of the birthmark on Alex's paw. 'Alakay?' she asked. The larger lion's fierce expression melted as he held up his own paw to reveal an identical birthmark. Alex couldn't believe it. He was reunited with his parents.

The four friends were excited to finally meet others of their kind. Marty felt right at home with the herd of zebras - they were cracka-lackin'!

Melman couldn't believe it when the other giraffes told him they didn't have a doctor. 'What if you catch a cold?' he asked.

'We go to the dying holes,' one of them replied. The giraffes all agreed that Melman could be their new doctor.

'Manhattan is short of two things. Parking and hippos.' Gloria explained, as handsome Moto Moto approached her. Gloria swooned. A boyfriend, at last.

Eager to impress his parents, Alex told them he was the king of New York. Everyone was thrilled, except Makunga, who wanted to be alpha lion. He came up with a nasty plan to get rid of Alex by entering him in the Rite of Passage ceremony.

Meanwhile, the penguins had a plan of their own to get materials to rebuild the plane. It was called Operation Tourist Trap. Private lay down in the road as a tour truck approached. Then, thud! The poor tour guide thought he had hit Private, and the tourists leaped out to help him, while the other penguins drove off with the truck!

Just as they were about to make a clean getaway, an angry Nana reared up behind them. Skipper braked sharply and she flew on to the road. Unhurt, she led the other tourists into the jungle. 'I'm not going to stay out in the open and get attacked by more animals,' she said. 'I'm too old to die.'

'**S**o, little cub scouts. Just remember, a great dance performance comes from the heart,' said Alex as the cubs giggled at him. Then Makunga sloped over and explained that Alex needed to choose a competitor for the Rite of Passage. 'If it was me out there, I'd choose Teetsi,' he said, with a wicked grin. As the gigantic Teetsi unfurled himself and strode into the ring, Zuba felt proud of his son's bold choice.

'Let's dance,' Teetsi roared.

And Alex did, as his parents watched in horror, unable to understand why he wasn't fighting. SLAM! Teetsi floored Alex with a single swipe. When Makunga insisted the failed Alex should be banished, Zuba chose to leave the pride rather than abandon his son. Finally, Makunga became leader of the pride.

The four friends met at the plane repair site. Not all of them were enjoying Africa. Alex couldn't believe he had failed the Rite of Passage, while Melman wanted to tell the others that he was about to die from witch doctor's disease. Nearly everyone thought they should fly back to New York immediately. But Gloria had just arranged a hot date with Moto Moto and was loving Africa. Jealous Melman started a loud row with Gloria and they both stormed off.

Alex was confused by his friends' behaviour but even more confused to see a second Marty! The zebra he had been talking to wasn't his old friend at all.

'You're saying there's nothing unique about me?' Marty asked, hurt that Alex couldn't recognise him. It was true. Alex couldn't tell him apart from the other zebras, so Marty left to be with the herd.

King Julien and Maurice found Melman sulking in his dying hole. 'I probably only have another two days left to live,' he told them.

'But there must be something you want to do before you die,' King Julien said.

When Melman confessed that he loved Gloria, the lemurs insisted he tell her. 'What are you afraid of?' Maurice asked. 'You're going to die anyway.'

Melman ran to the water hole where he found Moto Moto and Gloria on a romantic date. He confronted Moto Moto.

'You better treat this lady like a queen,' he declared, 'that's what I would do if I were you. But I'm not. So you do it.' Then, he walked away, leaving Gloria speechless.

Outside the reserve, something even stranger was happening. With a loud clump, the final log fell into place, blocking the river. The tourists' dam was complete and Nana could finally have her bath.

Downstream, a glum giraffe stared at the dried up water hole. The animals began to panic. How could they survive without water? They turned to the new alpha lion, Makunga. 'I'm afraid there is only one solution,' he said. 'We fight for it.'

Alex overheard everyone talking and knew what he had to do. He decided to travel upstream, off the reserve, and find out what had happened to the water.

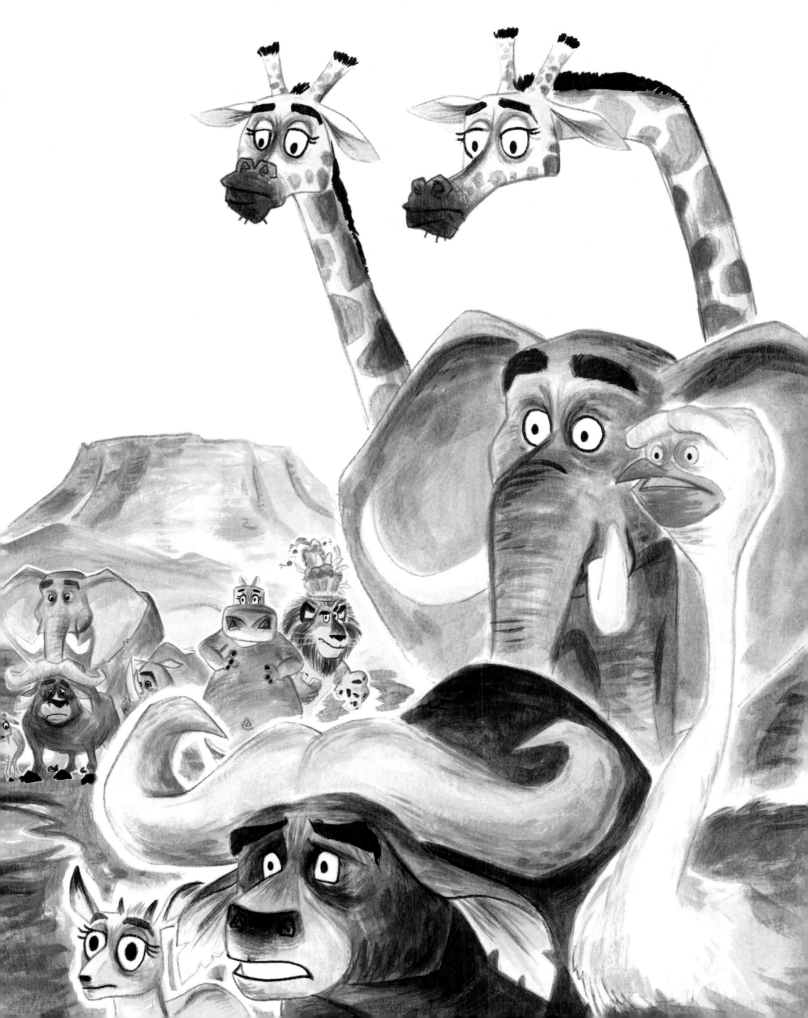

King Julien had his own idea for how to fix the water hole. 'All I need is someone who would like to go in the volcano and get eaten by the water gods,' he declared.

Melman raised his hand to volunteer. 'I'll do it,' he said.

Gloria rushed up to stop Melman, who stood on the edge of the volcano. Suddenly, the ground beneath him crumbled and Melman plunged towards the hot lava. Gloria dived forwards and caught him.

They stared into each others' eyes. 'It's crazy to think that I had to go half way 'round the world to find out that the perfect guy for me lived right next door.' Gloria said, hugging Melman.

Alex eventually found Marty in the herd of zebras and apologised to him. So Marty agreed to join Alex and they quickly discovered an enormous dam. Peering over the top, they saw Nana's tourist camp.

Suddenly, some hungry tourists spotted them. Alex and Marty fled through the jungle but Alex was caught in a trap. Marty kept running to try and get help.

'Let me go, please.' Alex pleaded, as the tourists tied him to a long pole and placed him over a cooking pit.

'Now, how about a nice lion casserole?' Nana asked the tourists.

With a roar, Zuba burst into the clearing and slashed the ropes binding Alex with his claws. The tourists moved in to attack. 'No, dad! They're New Yorkers - they are just rude and frightened!' Alex explained, leaping in front of him and striking a pose.

'What are you doing, son?' Zuba asked.

'The only thing I know how to do!' he replied.

As he danced, the tourists recognised him. 'It's Alex the lion! From the zoo!' they exclaimed. Zuba was stunned as the crowd dropped their weapons and applauded. His feet began to tap, and before he knew it, he was dancing, too!

But Nana was still hungry. As she grabbed a gun, the penguins' plane flew overhead and a chain of monkeys scooped Alex and Zuba into a barrel. The penguins swung the plane around and headed for the dam where Nana stood, ready to fight. With a giant smash, the dam broke, releasing the water back into the river.

The animals back at the water hole cheered as the water gushed towards them, with Alex and Zuba riding the wave in their barrel. 'My son! He saved us all!' Zuba cried to the crowd.

But there was one final surprise. Nana hopped out of the barrel, saw Makunga with her missing handbag and chased him across the reserve.

The animals celebrated around the water hole. Zuba led the pride again, Gloria and Melman had found love and Alex had earned his parents' respect by dancing instead of fighting.

It was the perfect excuse to throw a party!

Other exciting Madagascar books to collect!

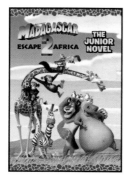

**Madagascar:
Escape 2 Africa –
THE JUNIOR NOVEL**

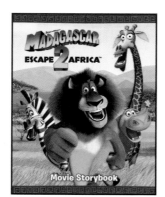

**Madagascar:
Escape 2 Africa –
MOVIE STORYBOOK**

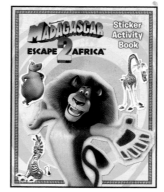

**Madagascar:
Escape 2 Africa –
STICKER ACTIVITY BOOK**

**Madagascar:
Escape 2 Africa –
COLOURING POSTER PAD**

**Madagascar: Escape 2 Africa –
WIPE CLEAN ACTIVITY BOOK**

**Madagascar: Escape 2 Africa –
SOUND BOOK**

**Madagascar: Escape 2 Africa –
JIGSAW BOOK**

**Madagascar:
Escape 2 Africa –
MAGNET BOOK**

**Madagascar:
Escape 2 Africa –
Father & Son
Save the Day**

**Madagascar:
Escape 2 Africa –
Air Penguin**

**Madagascar:
Escape 2 Africa –
POCKET LIBRARY**